To my children and all those who believe in unicorns — AD
To my children, Clare and Max — JB

Picture Window Books are published by Capstone,
1710 Roe Crest Drive, North Mankato, Minnesota 56003
www.mycapstone.com

Library of Congress Cataloging-in-Publication Data
Names: Darlison, Aleesah, author. | Brailsford, Jill, illustrator.
Title: Ellabeth's light / by Aleesah Darlison; illustrated by Jill Brailsford.
Description: North Mankato, Minnesota : Picture Window Books, [2017] |
    Series: Unicorn riders | Summary: When the kingdom is hit by unnaturally
    wild weather, Ellabeth and the other the Unicorn Riders find that the cause
    is a lost weather sprite called Lumi who has become separated from the
    retired wizard Kai Liang—but before they can take him home and calm the
    weather they must gather his four elements and defeat the boy Gelsan who
    works for the evil Lord Valerian.
Identifiers: LCCN 2016037803| ISBN 9781479565511 (library binding) |
    ISBN 9781479565597 (paperback)
Subjects: LCSH: Unicorns-Juvenile fiction. | Magic—Juvenile fiction.
    |Spirits—Juvenile fiction. | Weather—Juvenile fiction. |Wizards—Juvenile
    fiction. | Adventure stories. | CYAC: Unicorns—Fiction. | Magic—Fiction.
    | Spirits—Fiction. | Weather--Fiction. | Wizards—Fiction. | Adventure
    and adventurers—Fiction. | GSAFD: Adventure fiction. | LCGFT: Action and
    adventure fiction.
Classification: LCC PZ7.1.D333 Ej 2017 | DDC 813.6 [Fic] —dc23
LC record available at https://lccn.loc.gov/2016037803

Editor: Nikki Potts
Designer: Kayla Rossow
Art Director: Juliette Peters
Production Specialist: Kathy McColley
The illustrations in this book were created by Jill Brailsford.

Cover design by Walker Books Australia Pty Ltd
Cover images: Rider, symbol, and unicorns © Gillian Brailsford 2011;
lined paper © iStockphoto.com/Imageegaml;
parchment © iStockphoto.com/Peter Zelei

The illustrations for this book were created with black pen,
pencil, and digital media.

Design Element: Shutterstock: Slanapotam

Printed and bound in China.
010377F17

UNICORN RIDERS

Ellabeth's Light

Aleesah Darlison

Illustrations by
Jill Brailsford

PICTURE WINDOW BOOKS
a capstone imprint

Willow & Obecky

Willow's symbol
- a violet—represents being watchful and faithful

Uniform color
- green

Unicorn
- Obecky has a black opal horn.
- She has the gifts of healing and strength.

Ellabeth & Fayza

Ellabeth's symbol
- a hummingbird—represents energy, persistence, and loyalty

Uniform color
- red

Unicorn
- Fayza has an orange topaz horn.
- She has the gift of speed and can also light the dark with her golden magic.

Quinn & Ula

Quinn's symbol
- a butterfly—represents change and lightness

Uniform color
- blue

Unicorn
- Ula has a ruby horn.
- She has the gift of speaking with Quinn using mind-messages.
- She can also sense danger.

Krystal & Estrella

Krystal's symbol
- a diamond—represents perfection, wisdom, and beauty

Uniform color
- purple

Unicorn
- Estrella has a pearl horn.
- She has the gift of enchantment.

The Unicorn Riders' World

Kingdom of Obeera

Kingdom of Lillius

Kingdom of Korsitaan

Maylee

Trope

Mountains of Trope

Sea of Desperation

Trilby

Kingdom of Avamay

Effervescent Falls

Palace

UR Compound

City of Keydell

Desperation Point

Stillmet

Tivia Wood

Cardamon

Miramar

Arlen

Hot Springs

Lake Feather-Bay

Islands of Ipsus

Merroweed

Gringot

Woods of Shanahan

Dove Mountain

Kingdom of Haartsfeld

Dagger Mountains

Gulf of Curzon

Idle Bay

Sea of Angels

The Unicorn Riders of Avamay

Under the guidance of their leader, Jala, the Unicorn Riders and their magical unicorns protect the Kingdom of Avamay from the threats of evil Lord Valerian.

Decades ago, Lord Valerian forcefully took over the neighboring kingdom of Obeera. He began capturing every magical creature across the eight kingdoms. Luckily, King Perry saved four of Avamay's unicorns. He asked the unicorns to help protect Avamay. And that's when ordinary girls were chosen to be the first Unicorn Riders.

A Rider is chosen when her name and likeness appear in The Choosing Book, which is guarded by Jala. It holds the details of all the past, present, and future Riders. No one can see who the future Riders will be until it is time for a new Rider to be chosen. Only then will The Choosing Book display her details.

• CHAPTER 1 •

ELLABETH SWUNG ONTO FAYZA'S back and cantered across the paddock toward the stream. It was a gorgeous day for a ride. The sun was shining. Birds twittered and flittered overhead. The trees shifted in the breeze that smelled of gardenias and frangipanis.

"What a beautiful part of Avamay this is," Ellabeth whispered into her unicorn's ear as they galloped along. "Come on, girl. Let's go faster so we can explore more of it!"

Fayza whinnied excitedly. Her hooves flew over the grass as she carried her Rider along. Ellabeth, who trusted Fayza completely, closed her eyes to fully enjoy the thrill of the wind through her hair and the feeling of her unicorn racing beneath her.

Ellabeth and the other Unicorn Riders were staying at a country house near Avamay's hot springs. The girls had been on several dangerous missions recently, trying to protect the land of Avamay from the evil Lord Valerian. Queen Heart ruled the land and was grateful for the Rider's help. She felt the Riders deserved a break, and she'd offered her gorgeous estate for them to stay at. The Riders had spent several days enjoying the hot springs, which had worked wonders mending their aching muscles and lifting their spirits.

As she raced along on Fayza, Ellabeth felt something change in the air. Shadows darkened and the breeze turned cold.

Ellabeth shivered as goosebumps rose on her arms.

How come it's so cool all of a sudden? she wondered. *And what happened to the birds?*

Ellabeth turned her head to listen. The world had gone silent. Overhead, storm clouds shut out the blue sky. Heavy rain drummed across the paddock toward her.

"Let's get you into the stables," Ellabeth said. "Quick, girl."

With Fayza's speed magic swirling out from her topaz horn, Ellabeth and Fayza raced back to the house.

The other unicorns, Obecky, Ula, and Estrella, were out in the paddock. Moments ago, they'd been grazing on the long grass. The sudden onset of the storm now had them whinnying nervously.

An angry rumble of thunder was followed by a lightning flash. Ellabeth urged all four unicorns toward the stables. They galloped inside as the other Riders arrived wearing raincoats.

"Are you okay?" Krystal asked.

"I'm fine," Ellabeth said. "This storm is a bit frightening though."

"It's come out of nowhere," Quinn agreed as she and the other girls dried off their unicorns and settled them into their stalls.

Ellabeth gazed out the stable doors. The rain fell in thick sheets, blocking out the house. The wind howled, making the roof rattle and the walls shake. "It sure is odd for this time of year," she said.

"It's just a freak storm," Willow said as she filled Obecky's basket with fresh oats.

"I hope that's all it is and not a sign of something bad to come," Krystal said as she patted Estrella to reassure her. Storms always made her flighty.

When the rain finally stopped, the Riders trudged back to the house. Ellabeth spotted something fluttering beneath a gardenia bush. Just recently the plant had been covered with creamy, fragrant flowers. But the storm had knocked every last petal off so they now lay in a thick sludge on the ground.

"What's that?" Ellabeth asked as she bent down for a closer look. "Oh, no!"

Ellabeth crawled beneath the bush. Flowers plastered her hands and legs. She caught a drenched, injured bird lying there and brought it into the open.

"It's Belmont," Quinn gasped. "And he's hurt."

Belmont was a messenger falcon. He flew all over

13

Avamay delivering messages for Queen Heart and helping the Riders.

"What's he doing out in this storm?" Krystal asked.

"He probably got caught and didn't have time to find shelter," Ellabeth said. She held the bird close, trying to warm him. "He must have been blown under there."

"Such a brave bird," Quinn said stroking the falcon's head.

Belmont screeched weakly.

"Has he got a message?" Willow asked.

Ellabeth checked the leather strap tied around Belmont's leg. "Yes," replied Ellabeth.

"Let's get him and the message inside," Willow said, eyeing the sky as lightning sliced the clouds once more. "Looks like this storm isn't over yet."

Ellabeth shook her head. "All is not right in Avamay. I'm sure of it," she said.

• CHAPTER 2 •

"RIDERS!" JALA EXCLAIMED AS she ran to the girls, hugging them. Jala was the Unicorn Riders' leader. "I was so worried. This weather is incredibly fierce," she said. "Is everyone all right?"

Ellabeth showed Jala the bird. "Poor Belmont caught the worst of the storm," Ellabeth said. "He's hurt badly."

"Looks like he's in shock," Jala said. "Queen Heart will be most upset when she hears about this. Bring him over by the fire. The warmth will do him good."

While Ellabeth held Belmont by the fire, stroking him soothingly, Jala fetched fresh water and a meal of minced meat, which she fed him by hand.

I couldn't bear it if anything happened to Belmont, Ellabeth thought. *I hope he's going to be okay.*

"Willow," Jala said. "Why don't you read the message Belmont brought with him."

Willow sat beside Ellabeth and Belmont as she opened the small square of notepaper. Krystal and Quinn gathered nearby.

"It's from villagers in Cardamon," Willow said, glancing at Ellabeth.

Ellabeth's hand flew to her chest in alarm. "Not my parents?" she said.

Cardamon Valley was Ellabeth's home. Before her name had appeared in The Choosing Book and she became a Unicorn Rider, Ellabeth had lived on a farm in the valley with her parents and her five sisters.

"No," Willow said. "It's from a village farther south called Raleena."

She held up the note and read:

> Dear Queen Heart and courageous
> Unicorn Riders,
>
> Please hear our plea. Our valley has been
> plagued by wild storms. Rain, hail, and now snow
> have pounded our homes for days.
>
> We have never witnessed weather like this
> before. People are injured and sick. Our animals
> are suffering terribly. Crops have been ruined.
> We possess little food because we have just
> gotten through winter. Our stores are low.
> Please find out what is causing this terrible
> weather. Help us!
>
> In desperation,
> The villagers of Raleena

"Sounds like they're seeing strange weather like we did today," Quinn said.

"Belmont was lucky to have made it through," Ellabeth said. "We should ride to Raleena right away and find out what's happening there."

"But we're under strict instructions from Queen Heart to relax and recuperate," Krystal pointed out.

Willow frowned. "I'd like to rest a little longer, too, but Ellabeth is right," she said. "We can't let these people suffer."

"I agree," Jala said. "I can send a message to Queen Heart once Belmont recovers. I'm sure she'll understand. In the meantime, you girls must ready the unicorns and set out for Raleena."

"Shall I see if Ula can sense what's happening in Cardamon?" Quinn asked.

"Sure," Willow said. "That would be helpful."

Quinn closed her eyes to communicate with her unicorn. Ellabeth admired the way Quinn and Ula connected, and Ula's special skill of sending mind-messages to Quinn. The unicorn's ability to predict dangerous situations before they occurred had saved the Riders on many occasions.

After several minutes, Quinn opened her eyes. She rubbed her temples. "We tried hard, but Ula can't see anything. The storm is blocking her view," said Quinn.

"Never mind," Willow said, squeezing her hand. "We'll go and investigate anyway."

While the Riders prepared the unicorns, Jala collected supplies for the Riders to take in their packs. They were soon ready to leave and gathered at the front of the house.

Ellabeth was secretly glad they were heading out on an adventure. Three idle days in the house had made her more impatient than usual.

"Remember to stick together," Jala said, as she said goodbye to the Riders. "This mission sounds like it will be a dangerous one."

"We'll be fine," Willow said as she smiled down from her seat on Obecky. "We have each other and our unicorns."

"I know," Jala said smiling. "But that doesn't stop me from worrying."

Willow raised her hand. "Do we ride as one?" she asked.

"We ride as one!" The Riders cheered as they galloped after Willow.

Ellabeth smiled as she rode beside her friends, perfectly content despite the dangers that might lie ahead.

The Riders reached Cardamon Valley well into the night. The weather steadily worsened as they drew nearer to Raleena and the snow swirled around them, making it almost impossible to see.

It's a good thing we brought our coats, Ellabeth thought as she snuggled deeper into the warm folds of her fur-trimmed jacket. *We'd freeze without them.*

By the light of the moon, the Riders saw the devastation the storm had caused. Trees had been toppled by ferocious winds. Rivers were frozen over. Snow was piled thickly all around.

Ellabeth's mouth gaped in shock. "It never snows here," she said. "Everything looks so strange covered in white."

"It's a springtime wonderland," Quinn joked.

"That's one way to put it," Willow said as she shook her head in disbelief.

"Is the snow real or is it an illusion?" Krystal asked.

Ellabeth slipped down off Fayza to grasp a handful of snow. "It's cold, that's for sure. And soft. Makes

a great snowball," Ellabeth said as she tossed it at Krystal.

"What was that for?" Krystal shrieked.

"*You* are a Krystal," Ellabeth said cheekily. "And snowflakes are crystals. You belong together."

"I don't know what gets into you sometimes," Krystal said with a giggle.

"Hey, what's that?" Quinn asked pointing to a glowing orange light.

"Probably someone's house," Willow said.

"No, it's moving," Ellabeth said, mounting Fayza and urging her forward. "Come on. Let's see what it is."

• CHAPTER 3 •

ELLABETH TOOK OFF AFTER the shimmering light. She was fascinated by the rapidly moving beacon and wondered if it might somehow be connected to the strange weather patterns. The other Riders struggled to keep up because Fayza was so fast.

Ellabeth was soon far ahead of the others. Lost in the chase, she remained completely focused on the light as it zipped and dashed everywhere. It bounded from the treetops to the ground and then back into the trees.

How peculiar, Ellabeth thought. *It looks alive.*

As she closed in on the light, Ellabeth jumped off Fayza. The snow was freezing, wet, and up to her knees, but she didn't stop. The light flickered, tempting her to come closer. She carefully reached out her hand.

The light zipped to the right. She was sure she heard giggling.

"Are you laughing at me?" Ellabeth asked, steaming with anger despite the cold. "I'll show you," she said.

She stumbled through the snow, chasing the light. It seemed to be tiring because it began to move more slowly. But it was still too quick for Ellabeth.

Maybe I should try coaxing it instead? she thought.

"Come here, little light," Ellabeth murmured. "I won't hurt you."

The light landed right in Ellabeth's hands. She barely stopped herself from squealing in shock.

The light changed from orange to pink and then purple as it made a purring sound.

Now that Ellabeth was close to it, she could tell it wasn't just a light. A tiny transparent figure stood inside the glow. It looked like a tiny goblin with oversized eyes, large lips, and big ears.

"What's going on?" Krystal called running through the snow with Willow and Quinn to where Ellabeth stood. She marveled at the purring light. "Are you all right?" Krystal asked.

"Isn't this amazing?" Ellabeth said.

"Bzzzzz!" said the light.

"What are you?" Ellabeth asked.

"Gig-gig-gig," the creature said. He held his hands together and rocked back and forth looking nervous.

"Oh, my goodness," Quinn breathed. "I know what this is. I remember reading about it in one of Jala's books. It's a weather sprite."

Willow frowned. "A what?" she asked.

"A weather sprite," Quinn said. "There's only one in all Avamay, and it hasn't been seen for ages. It's cared for by Kai Liang. He's the wizard who used to work for King Perry, Queen Heart's father. After King Perry died, Kai Liang retired. No one has seen him since."

"Zip-zip-zip," the sprite said stabbing his finger at the Riders.

"Perhaps Kai Liang died," Quinn said. "That might be why the sprite got loose. It could have caused this destructive weather."

"It's one naughty sprite if it did," Krystal said.

"And dangerous," said Willow as she crossed her arms. "Can it talk?"

"Can you talk, sprite?" Ellabeth asked sternly.

"Grig-grig-grig," replied the sprite.

"Stop that!" Ellabeth snapped. "What are you doing here?"

"It looks scared," Quinn said.

Ellabeth stroked the sprite's shimmering outline. "It's all right. We won't hurt you," she said. "We work for Queen Heart."

The sprite's transparent glow turned deep purple. Its purring grew louder.

"That's working," Willow said. "Keep doing that."

"Please, will you talk to us?" Ellabeth asked.

The sprite stood on tiptoe and whispered into Ellabeth's ear.

"That tickles," she giggled.

"Did it say anything?" Willow asked.

"Yes," Ellabeth said. "He was traveling with Kai Liang on their way back from visiting the wizard's son, Tellarian. Because Kai Liang is getting old, he wanted to pass on his knowledge to Tellarian, but Tellarian wasn't interested. This little guy wandered off while Kai Liang

was napping. He got lost. Ever since, he's been afraid, lonely, and desperate to return home."

"Did he make this mess?" Krystal asked.

The sprite whispered in Ellabeth's ear and then gazed at Krystal with wide, innocent eyes.

"He doesn't know what else to do," Ellabeth explained. "He's a weather sprite. All he can do to show that he's unhappy or sad or angry is to change color, which in turn can affect the weather. Sometimes in a bad way."

"So the little thing *did* create this havoc?" Krystal said staring at the destruction the sprite had caused. "How is it possible?"

The weather sprite puffed his chest out. "I may be small, but I'm very powerful," he announced proudly.

"How come you're talking so well now when before you could only make funny sounds?" Quinn asked looking puzzled.

"I get tongue-tied around new people," said the sprite. "You seem nice though. Am I right?"

"Of course we're nice," Ellabeth said. "You don't have to worry about us hurting you."

"Thank you," he said. "I just want to see Kai Liang again."

"We're going to get you home as soon as we can," Willow said. "But that doesn't mean we're happy that you've endangered lives." She wagged a finger at him.

"I'm sorry," the sprite whispered, glowing yellow.

"What's your name?" Ellabeth asked.

"Luminari," the sprite replied. "You can call me Lumi if you like."

"I hope the people of Raleena are willing to forgive you," Willow said. "How are we going to return you to Kai Liang? Where does he live?"

"He's supposed to live in Zenna Castle, deep in the Dagger Mountains," Quinn said. "Down south."

"There's just one teensy-tiny problem," Lumi said. He held his fingers close together, as if measuring something minute. "You can't take me home until we collect my elements."

"What elements?" Krystal asked.

The sprite looked so guilty that Ellabeth couldn't help feeling sorry for him. He held up a small leather pouch.

"The elements I usually keep in here," said Lumi. "I cast them to the four compass points when I was upset. If we don't get them back, the weather will keep going crazy."

"That sounds dangerous," Quinn said.

Willow's eyebrows scrunched together. "Did he say *four* compass points?" she asked.

Ellabeth winced. "I'm afraid so," she said.

"Okay. Right," Willow said. She took a deep breath. "First, we'll visit Raleena to assure the villagers that we're taking care of things, and hopefully the weather will be back to normal soon. Then we'll start collecting his elements."

"What exactly are these elements we're looking for?" Ellabeth asked.

"Earth, water, air, and fire," Lumi said.

"Do we need to collect them in that order?" Ellabeth asked.

Lumi nodded. "I need all of my elements for my powers to work properly," he replied. "And the elements must be united in their proper order or else the weather will never be right again. The elemental powers will fight each other and cause destruction across Avamay." Lumi held out his hands, appealing to the Riders. "I feel terrible," he said. "I wasn't thinking straight when I threw them away."

Willow rubbed her forehead. Ellabeth could see she was worried. "Precisely where did you throw each of them?" Willow asked.

"I'm not sure," the sprite said. "I was terribly upset, you see. All I remember is the general direction."

"Okay, so, earth," Quinn said. "Can you remember anything about that one?"

Lumi scratched his chin. "I can sense the elements and feel what it is they have around them, even if they're not with me," he said. "When I think of the earth element, I sense something to do with caves."

"Caves?" Ellabeth asked tapping her chin thoughtfully. "That could be Cadric Mount near Bella Plains."

"I bet that's it," Willow said.

"Don't tell me I got something to do with geography right?" Ellabeth said.

"Jala would be so proud," Krystal teased.

"Is it safe at Cadric Mount?" Quinn asked looking concerned.

"I hope so," Willow said. "If not, this mission might be more dangerous than we imagined."

• CHAPTER 4 •

AFTER ASSURING THE PEOPLE of Raleena that they were working to solve the weather problems, the Riders set out for Cadric Mount. Using Fayza's speed magic to help them go faster, they galloped through the night enveloped by a honey-gold glow. Inside the golden light shone another smaller light. Lumi.

Ellabeth glanced down to admire the sprite as he perched on her shoulder where he could watch the world race by.

He looks so small and helpless, she thought. *I hope we can get him back to Kai Liang safely.*

"Cadric Mount is a large area, Lumi," Krystal said as they rode. "It's riddled with caves. Do you have any more clues to help us locate your earth element?"

"I'll feel its presence once I'm nearby," Lumi said. "Although, it will have wriggled deep underground where it feels most safe."

"I'm not sure that's very helpful information," Willow said.

"Oh, dear," Lumi sighed. "This is all my fault."

"Never mind," Ellabeth said, soothing the sprite. "We'll sort things out."

By sunrise, the friends had arrived at Cadric Mount. A long, narrow trail snaked through the surrounding hills, which were dotted with caves.

"Can you feel your earth element?" Ellabeth asked Lumi.

The sprite shook his head. "No, not yet," he replied.

"What about Ula?" Willow asked Quinn. "Can she see anything?"

"Ula's showing me a huge black, jagged rock," Quinn said. "It has one tree, an elm, on top. Below is a cave filled with crystals."

Willow's eyes lit up. "The Solitary Elm," she said. "We learned about that in our history lessons. That's where the Battle of Kellon-Rah was fought two centuries ago."

Lumi clapped his hands. "Yes, the Solitary Elm," he said. "It's becoming clearer in my mind. We're getting close."

"Ula showed me this path, too," Quinn said pointing to the trail.

"Ellabeth, you and Lumi lead," Willow said. "We'll follow."

Ellabeth led the way through the mountain pass. She gazed nervously up at the rock walls on either side of her. "Does anyone live here?" she asked.

"This place is so hot and dry that most people live underground or in the caves where it's cool," Quinn explained.

"Are they friendly?" Krystal asked.

"I'm not sure," Quinn replied.

The unicorns' footsteps echoed eerily through the silent canyon. They rounded a corner where the rock walls opened out to reveal a stream meandering over rocks and sand. Stunted bushes and grasses added color to the orange landscape.

"There's the Solitary Elm," Quinn said, pointing into the distance.

The Riders cantered toward the tree and then dismounted.

"I feel like we're being watched," Willow said as she glanced around. "Look, there's the cave entrance," she said pointing. "We'll have to take the unicorns with us, just in case."

Ellabeth led the others into the cave and underground. At first, the unicorns were hesitant, but their Riders soon calmed them. Fayza's light magic and Lumi's glow helped show the way.

The cave below the Solitary Elm was so big. Its ceiling towered high above them. As they traveled deeper into the cave, the temperature dropped dramatically.

Ellabeth shivered. "It's freezing in here," she said. She considered putting her coat back on, but Krystal tugged her arm, distracting her.

"Look how the limestone twinkles," Krystal said. "Isn't it breathtaking?"

From the ceiling, cream-and-caramel colored tentacles of limestone stretched to the ground where water pooled. Rising from the pools were spindly limestone stalagmites extending toward the ceiling. Some formations had been there so long they'd joined with the stalactites hanging from the ceiling to form thick columns.

"We're getting closer," Lumi said. He rapidly changed color in his excitement. The girls gasped in wonder as his colors played out across the glistening limestone.

Then they saw it. Sitting on top of a bulbous limestone formation was a shiny black crystal, shaped like an egg.

"My earth element," Lumi said.

Ellabeth reached out to grasp it, but the limestone was slippery and she accidentally knocked the element into a large pool of water.

The Riders and Lumi gasped.

"Sometimes I'm such a klutz," Ellabeth scolded herself. "Sorry, Lumi."

"Can you reach into the pond and get it?" Lumi asked.

Ellabeth kneeled down and put her hand into the pool. As she felt around for the element, her arm went deeper until the water was up to her shoulder. Beside her, Lumi wrung his hands together.

Ellabeth's fingers touched the element. As her hand closed around it, something grabbed her arm.

"Help!" Ellabeth's screams echoed throughout the cave. "Something's got my arm."

Krystal and Quinn ran to Ellabeth's aid. They tried holding her, but she was pulled farther into the pool.

"Obecky," Willow said, "use your magic to grip Ellabeth."

The unicorn obeyed. Gray-blue magic shimmered from her opal horn, covering Ellabeth.

"Good girl, now bring her up," Willow instructed.

It took all of Ellabeth's self-control not to cry. "My arm's hurting so much," she gasped. "It keeps twisting tighter."

"Stay calm," Quinn said. "Obecky won't let anything happen to you."

"All right," Ellabeth said as she took a deep breath. She still held the element, refusing to let it go, no matter how tightly her arm was squeezed.

Be brave, she told herself. *Be brave.*

Obecky stepped backward, dragging Ellabeth with her. The unicorn's muscles bulged and her magic whirled. Ellabeth felt the hold on her arm weaken. Obecky's magic was too strong for whatever held her. Soon the grasp on Ellabeth's arm was released. She fell back in a heap beside the pond.

"What *was* that?" Krystal asked.

"I don't think I want to know," Ellabeth said, rubbing her arm where it hurt.

Quinn pointed at the water. "Look!" she yelled.

A serpent-like coil rose above the water's surface then disappeared.

Ellabeth shuddered as she patted Obecky. "Thanks for saving me," she said. "I thought I was a goner."

"You're going to have a nice bruise," Willow said inspecting Ellabeth's arm. "Obecky, use your healing magic to soothe the pain."

As Obecky wove her magic, Ellabeth held up the earth element. "I guess this means one down, three to go," she said.

Willow gave Ellabeth a brief hug. "Well done for holding onto it," she said. "Now, let's get you out of here. This place gives me the creeps."

Krystal and the others led Ellabeth out of the cave.

"Where's Lumi?" Ellabeth asked.

"Oh, no!" Quinn gasped. "He's gone."

● CHAPTER 5 ●

"WE HAVE TO FIND LUMI," Ellabeth said as she swung up onto Fayza. "Let's go!"

Without waiting for the others, she raced along the trail searching for Lumi and calling his name. Up ahead, she saw a red light and urged Fayza to gallop faster. "I know you're tired, girl, but we can't give up now," Ellabeth said.

As the gap between her and the light narrowed, Ellabeth realized someone was carrying Lumi. He'd been kidnapped!

The thief — a boy — was running so fast, Ellabeth wondered if he was using magic. Whatever it was, he still wasn't fast enough to outrun Fayza.

Ellabeth jumped down and tackled the thief to the ground. "Got you!" she said.

The thief was strong, and he wasn't giving up without a fight. But Ellabeth was determined.

"Give him to me," said Ellabeth. She wrenched Lumi from the boy. The sprite turned purple and began purring in gratitude.

"Hey! Don't I know you?" Ellabeth demanded.

The sound of galloping hooves filled the night.

"You're going to be in trouble when Willow gets here," Ellabeth said.

"Too bad she missed me," the boy snarled before sprinting away.

"Hey!" Ellabeth yelled. She chased after him, but the gaps between the rocks allowed him the perfect getaway.

44

Ellabeth ran back to the others.

"That's the second time you've taken off without us, Ellabeth," Willow said. "We're meant to ride as one, remember?"

"I know," Ellabeth said. She was furious at herself for letting the thief escape. "I just couldn't bear the thought of losing Lumi. Are you all right?" she asked Lumi as she cradled him to her chest.

"I'm fine," Lumi replied. "Just a little shaken. I wish Kai Liang were here."

"What happened?" Quinn asked.

"He was taken," Ellabeth said. "I got him back, but the thief ran away."

"If you'd waited for us, that wouldn't have happened," Krystal said.

"If I'd waited, I might not have found Lumi," Ellabeth argued. "That boy was fast."

"Did you see who it was?" Willow asked.

"Gelsan," Ellabeth said. "The boy who works for Valerian."

"Then Lord Valerian is behind this for sure," Krystal said. "Gelsan was probably using his master's magic to help him run fast. How do you think they knew about Lumi?"

"Unfortunately, our nasty neighbor has spies everywhere," Willow said. "Perhaps one of them reported the strange weather patterns to him or spotted us with Lumi." She glanced over her shoulder suspiciously. "There may even be a chance they intercepted Jala's message to Queen Heart," she said.

"Oh, no!" Quinn exclaimed. She looked horrified. "Do you think Valerian has Belmont?"

"I hope not," Willow said. "But we're going to have to be careful from now on. Valerian's spies could be watching us right now."

"Why would Valerian want Lumi?" Ellabeth asked.

"You've seen how powerful the sprite is," Willow said. "And how destructive his weather forces are. If Valerian was able to control Lumi, imagine the devastation he could wreak on Avamay and its allies."

"I didn't mean to cause trouble," Lumi said sadly.

"We know," Ellabeth said as she hugged him. "It's not your fault." She handed him the earth element. "This might cheer you up."

Lumi smiled as he slipped the element inside the pouch slung over his shoulder. "Thank you, Ellabeth," he said.

"Where do you think Gelsan's gone?" Krystal asked.

"Possibly to get reinforcements," Willow said as she gnawed her thumbnail. "If Valerian wants something, he won't let it slip through his hands without a fight. This is not good. Quinn, can Ula see where the next element is?"

Quinn communicated with Ula. "It looks like Effervescent Falls," she said. "I remember it from when we were there working for Queen Heart to rebuild the town after the floods."

"That's it!" Lumi exclaimed, jumping up and down excitedly. "The element is hidden behind the waterfall."

"Keep your voice down!" Krystal hissed.

"We'll need to ride past Keydell to reach the falls," Willow said. "Someone should detour to the capital to let Queen Heart know what's happening and find out whether Belmont is safe. Any volunteers?" she asked.

Quinn raised her hand. "I'll do it," she said. "If there's danger, Ula will sense it beforehand."

"Good idea," Willow said. "When we near Keydell, make your detour. You can use Ula's magic to find us later. Let's go."

The race to Cadric Mount and lighting the cave to find the earth element had depleted Fayza's magic, so the girls could only travel at normal speed to Effervescent Falls. Ellabeth worried the whole time that they were being followed.

Deep in the night, they stopped near Trayneff. They set up camp in the forest for safety. They didn't light a fire and ate cold food from their packs. Then they curled up in their sleeping bags to rest.

Ellabeth kept Lumi in her uniform pocket so he wouldn't be spotted. The sprite was still fretting about his master. Every so often he would cause a shower of rain to fall, which made sleeping difficult. Ellabeth spent most of the night reassuring Lumi or putting up with the cold and the damp. She was glad when morning arrived so they could set out again. Fayza's magic had replenished overnight so they were able to travel swiftly once more.

Quinn left them midmorning to hurry on to Keydell. Ellabeth, Lumi, Krystal, and Willow reached Effervescent Falls around midday. They paused within the shelter of a group of trees.

Krystal squinted as she scanned the area. "There's no sign of Gelsan," she said.

"That's good," Willow said. "That waterfall looks dangerous enough. Look how fast it's flowing," she said, pointing at the waterfall.

"No one ever said this was going to be easy," Ellabeth said. She still felt guilty about failing to catch Gelsan. "Why don't you two stay here while Lumi and I go behind the waterfall?"

"Are you sure that's safe?" Lumi asked as he flickered pale green.

"I can't guarantee it," Ellabeth said. She tried not to laugh at the sprite's worried face. "But we've got to fetch your water element, right?"

Lumi gulped. "Yes," he replied.

"You'll need someone to hold your hand," Krystal said half-jokingly. "I'll come with you."

Relief washed over Ellabeth. "Thanks," she said. "That would be great."

"I'll watch the unicorns and keep a lookout," Willow said. "Now, be careful. Both sides of the pool are lined with slippery moss-covered rocks, too. They're dangerous for climbing. To get behind the waterfall, you're going to have to swim under it."

Ellabeth and Krystal removed their boots and tunics, leaving their leggings and undershirts on. They stepped into the pool and swam toward the waterfall. Lumi sat on Ellabeth's shoulder.

"Hold your breath," Ellabeth said. The girls dived under the flowing sheet of water. Lumi clung to Ellabeth's hair so he wouldn't get washed away. It was icy cold where the waterfall beat down dangerously with a swirling, churning motion. The girls had to kick hard and swim deep to avoid being pummeled by the downpour. All the way, Lumi's glow lit the way for them.

When they were safely past the waterfall, Ellabeth and Krystal swam upward, eventually emerging on the other side. Gasping for air, they climbed onto the rocks behind the waterfall. Using Lumi's light, they carefully made their way through the dark.

"I sense the water element," Lumi said, letting go of Ellabeth's hair. He flicked the water from himself and perched on her shoulder. "There," he said, pointing toward the rocks.

Ellabeth found a slit in the rock where Lumi pointed. She sat Lumi on the nearby rocks and pressed her eye against the gap. "I see it," she said. "It's aqua-colored and shaped like a star."

"That's it," Lumi said. "Can you reach it?"

Ellabeth tried slipping her hand through the gap. "No," she replied.

Krystal had no luck either.

Ellabeth bit her bottom lip, thinking. "What about flushing it out with water?" she said.

"It's worth a try," Krystal replied.

The girls scooped up handfuls of water and tipped them into the gap between the rocks. The chamber slowly filled.

"Just a little more . . . ," Ellabeth tossed a final handful into the opening. The element bobbed closer to the gap and then slid right through. It landed on a shiny wet rock beside the waterfall. Water gushed over the element, making it wobble precariously.

"Quick, Ellabeth! Grab it," Krystal gasped.

Ellabeth lunged toward the element with her hands outstretched. Her fingers were almost over the blue crystal when a large gush of water thundered down and washed the element into the pond below. Ellabeth fell to her knees, her hands bunched into fists. "No!" she yelled.

• CHAPTER 6 •

"WATCH LUMI," ELLABETH TOLD Krystal before diving headfirst through the waterfall. Her eyes never left the aqua-colored element as it tumbled into the depths below before coming to rest on a rock. To Ellabeth's surprise, the rock began to move. Then it grew a head and legs.

That's not a rock, she thought. *That's a turtle!*

Ellabeth tried to pluck the water element off the turtle's back, but the creature snapped at her. Its sharp jaws almost closed over her hands several times. Ellabeth dodged this way and that, trying to evade the turtle's snapping teeth to grab the element.

Finally, she saw her chance and grasped hold of the crystal. With lungs burning, she swam to the surface where she burst out of the water. "I found it!" she exclaimed.

Willow and Krystal rushed over to help her.

"Well done! That's two out of four," Willow said as she pulled Ellabeth onto her feet.

"You were under there for ages," Krystal said, hugging Ellabeth tight. "I searched for you as I swam back through the waterfall, but I couldn't see anything. I was so worried you weren't coming up."

"To be honest, so was I," Ellabeth said, laughing as she waded out of the pond. Fayza trotted over to nuzzle her Rider. "It's all right, girl. I'm fine."

"You and Krystal need to get dry," Willow said. "We'll light a fire and have something to eat."

"Is that safe?" Ellabeth asked.

"It's a risk we'll have to take," Willow said. "You need to get warm, and we all need food. I don't know about you, but I'm starving."

"Well, swimming does make me hungry," Ellabeth admitted.

"So does riding and dancing and talking and reading," Krystal joked, counting out the items on her hand.

"Okay," Ellabeth giggled. "I guess you've got me there."

Willow frowned. "Where's Lumi?" she asked.

"He was here a minute ago," Krystal said. "I brought him out from behind the waterfall with me."

Ellabeth froze, worried the sprite had been stolen again, until she spotted him beside the waterfall.

"There he is," said Ellabeth. "I'll go talk to him." She wandered over and handed Lumi the water crystal, which he slipped into his pouch.

"Thank you," he said softly.

"What's wrong?" asked Ellabeth.

The little sprite glowed blue and stared at the ground. His change in mood immediately affected the weather. Clouds formed overhead and tiny pinpricks of snow began falling. "I feel terrible for endangering everyone's lives, especially yours," he said. "I'm such a nuisance. Oh, I miss Kai Liang so much! I can't remember ever being without him." Ellabeth lifted Lumi up. He looked right into her eyes. "I can't help worrying about him," Lumi continued. "He's getting so old. He rarely travels any more, but he was determined to see his family one last time."

"If the Unicorn Riders have anything to do with it, you'll be reunited again soon," Ellabeth reassured the sprite.

Lumi purred and turned lavender. "You know exactly the right thing to say," he said.

"No one has ever told me that before," Ellabeth said, smiling warmly. "Usually, they tell me to stop talking or apologize for saying something wrong."

Ellabeth found herself opening up to Lumi. "I've always been too loud," she continued. "And a chatterbox according to my mother. Since becoming a Unicorn Rider, I've tried to work on my faults, but I don't always do a good job."

"You're doing a great job now," Ellabeth heard Willow's voice behind her. "I've never seen you so gentle before. Caring for Lumi has taught you new skills," said Willow.

"It's easy being kind to Lumi," Ellabeth said. "I like cheering him up. It's almost like having a little sister again. Besides, the gentler I am with him, the more beautiful his colors glow." She pointed at Lumi. "See? All you need do is treat him with a soft touch."

Ellabeth was silent for a moment before continuing. "Every day I try to be a better person, Willow," Ellabeth said. "I try to be like you or Quinn or Krystal. And let's face it, Krystal *is* perfect in every way."

Willow laughed. "Trust me. No one is perfect," she said. "And you shouldn't have to feel that way. Ever. You're a Unicorn Rider because you have your own special skills. The Choosing Book knew that when it selected you from all the girls in Avamay. We don't want you to be like Quinn or Krystal or me. We want you to be you."

Ellabeth blushed at Willow's compliment. "Thanks," she said. "That makes me feel much better." She sniffed the air and her tummy growled. "Hey, do I smell food? I'm starving," Ellabeth said.

"I believe you do," Willow said. "We checked the woods to make sure we were alone. Krystal lit a fire and is cooking us a quick meal. Come on. Let's eat."

The Riders devoured the fried mushrooms and toasted oat cakes Krystal had prepared for them.

"I wonder how Quinn's doing," Ellabeth said.

"Did someone mention my name?"

"Quinn!" Ellabeth, Willow, and Krystal greeted Quinn as she appeared through the trees and slid down off Ula.

"Thank goodness you're safe," Willow said.

"I told you Ula would look after me," Quinn said.

"What happened? Did you tell Queen Heart about the sprite? And that we saw Gelsan?" Krystal asked.

"I did," Quinn said. "Queen Heart has posted extra guards around the palace for security. Plus, she's sending a regiment of her best soldiers north to the Avamayan border. They're going to make sure Lord Valerian isn't trying to invade again in the hope of seizing Lumi himself."

"What about Belmont?" Krystal asked. "Is he okay?"

"He's safe at the palace," Quinn assured them. "Queen Heart is keeping him inside for the time being."

"Good idea," Ellabeth said.

"I see you've found the second element," Quinn said, nodding at Lumi who was sitting by the fire admiring his earth and water elements. "Where to now?" she asked.

Willow studied the sprite. "I'm hoping Lumi can tell us that," she said.

• CHAPTER 7 •

"THE NEXT ELEMENT IS AIR," Lumi replied. "My senses tell me it's south of here. I feel sunlight and wind and . . ." He shook his head. "I can't pick up anything else."

"Poor Lumi," Ellabeth said turning to Quinn. "Maybe Ula can help?"

"Sure. Let's give it a try," Quinn agreed.

As Quinn mind-messaged Ula, magic whirled from the unicorn's horn. "There's a narrow sandy beach," Quinn murmured. "Lumi's right. The sun is shining there. I know where it is. It's Idle Bay."

"Wow, that's far away," Krystal said.

"It sure is," Willow agreed. "I think we'll rest here tonight and set out tomorrow."

"The quicker we get to Idle Bay, the quicker we can move on and find the third element," Ellabeth argued.

"Don't be so impatient," Willow said. "We need rest, otherwise we'll just end up exhausted and be no good to anyone. So, like I said, let's camp here tonight and head out in the morning."

Ellabeth hated being called impatient, though part of her knew Willow was right. "Okay," she mumbled.

The girls and Lumi settled in for the night, taking turns to keep watch in case Lord Valerian's henchmen were lurking, ready to steal the sprite. The last thing they wanted was for Lumi to fall into Lord Valerian's hands and be used to create more havoc.

Once more, Ellabeth was glad when morning came and they could set out. It was a long ride to Idle Bay. Even with Fayza's speed magic, it took a day to get there. First they went over the plains west of Keydell, then through the mountains spanning southern Avamay, and finally to the ocean.

When the Riders galloped into Idle Bay in the afternoon, they found a beach of white sand stretching as far as they could see.

"There's nothing here but sand," Krystal observed. "Are we sure this is where the air element is?"

Lumi rubbed his temples. "It's here," he said. "I can feel it, but the signal is weak." He paced the beach, his shoulders hunched as he turned pale blue. The wind picked up with Lumi's thoughtful mood, sending a frosty blast swirling around the group.

Ellabeth gazed at the ocean. "What about there, Lumi?" Ellabeth asked as she indicated a rocky island not far from the shore. "Granite Island."

"Ula's sending me a mind-message," Quinn said. "She says the island is hiding a secret."

"Does she mean the element?" Willow asked.

"No," Quinn replied. "It's something *living*."

"Seals maybe?" Krystal suggested. "Granite Island is well known as a seal breeding ground."

"Is it?" Ellabeth asked. "I never knew."

"Like I always tell you," Krystal said, laughing, "you should pay attention in class."

"Ha-ha," Ellabeth said. She was too worried about finding the air element to rise to Krystal's bait. "I hope you're right though. That it's only seals out there."

"What if it's Gelsan or Valerian's spies waiting to ambush us?" Willow asked. "You never know when they're going to turn up."

"Maybe they've been following us all along," Krystal said. "Gelsan is pretty crafty."

The Riders murmured in agreement.

"Can Ula see anything else?" Willow asked.

"I'm afraid that's it," Quinn said.

"Lumi, can you feel the element out there?" Ellabeth asked.

Lumi stretched his hands toward Granite Island. "I think so. Yes," he said.

"How are we going to get out there?" Willow asked as she glanced up and down the coastline. "There isn't a boat in sight."

"Krystal and Quinn can stay here to keep a lookout while you and I take Obecky and Fayza to the island," Ellabeth said. "They can combine their strength and speed magic to make them swim fast and strong."

Willow nodded. "That just might work," she said.

Ellabeth glowed with pride, ecstatic that Willow liked her idea. She placed Lumi on her shoulder. "Let's go then," she said.

Obecky's gray-blue magic entwined with Fayza's honey-gold magic as they swam to the island, carrying their Riders.

"Do you think there are sharks?" Ellabeth asked.

Lumi shuddered. "Oh, I hope not," he replied.

"There are bound to be some sharks," Willow said, shooting Ellabeth a stiff smile. "But hopefully we won't meet any, right?"

"Right," Ellabeth said, laughing nervously. "Keep swimming, girl," she encouraged Fayza. "That's it, nice and steady."

When they reached the island, the unicorns stepped out of the water and up onto the rocks. Ellabeth and Willow glanced around, cautious after Ula's warning.

The island appeared deserted.

"That wasn't so bad, was it?" Willow said. "I can't see any seals though."

A loud roar sounded nearby. Lumi shivered and squeaked. Ellabeth hid him in her pocket. Thunder and lightning cracked overhead, brought on by Lumi's fear.

"I think that's what Ula warned us about," Willow said. Her hand trembled as she pointed to a dark shape moving toward them.

Ellabeth's eyes bulged as a huge shape loomed over them. It was a monster. It was tall, gray, and fat with razor-sharp teeth. Ellabeth thought it resembled an overgrown sea slug.

The monster roared again and struck at Willow.

"No!" Ellabeth screamed.

Willow was flung backward. She hit her head on a rock and lay unmoving on the ground. Ellabeth feared she might have been killed.

"Obecky and Fayza, stay with Willow," Ellabeth said. The unicorns obeyed. Obecky nudged her Rider's limp body.

Ellabeth turned to face the monster, which was now moving toward her. She took out her lasso and stood in a defensive pose. Her heart was thumping in her chest. Her hands were slick with sweat, and her knees trembled.

The gigantic creature rose higher in the air and bellowed.

Ellabeth glared. "You hurt my friend," she said. Her words sounded far braver than she felt. "Now you're going to pay." She swung her lasso.

The beast made a noise that sounded like laughter.

Ellabeth's temper flared. Her cheeks burned with anger. She stepped forward, her rope twirling. The monster advanced, banging its tail like a club.

"Stop right now!" Ellabeth shouted. "Stop or you'll regret it!"

The monster halted. "Who are you to tell me what to do?" it asked.

Ellabeth was relieved when she heard the monster speak.

If I can communicate with it, I might be able to reason with it. Perhaps, I won't have to use my lasso after all, she thought, slotting it back onto her belt.

"Is this the way you treat all your guests?" she asked.

"When they come to dinner, it is," the monster snarled. "Now, start running, little mouse. We'll play some more, and then I'm going to eat you."

● CHAPTER 8 ●

ELLABETH STOOD WITH HER hands on her hips. "I'm not a mouse," she said. "My name is Ellabeth Crisp, and I'm a Unicorn Rider. Why would you want to eat me when I protect all of Avamay's creatures, including you? You should be my friend."

"Friends?" The monster asked, appearing confused. "I have no friends. I'm forever hated and hunted. Killing is the only way I can protect myself."

"Do you really think you need to protect yourself from me?" Ellabeth appealed to the monster. "I won't hurt you, I promise."

"Then why are you here?" the monster asked.

"I'm looking for something my friend lost," Ellabeth said. "Have you seen a small crystal?"

"No," the monster grumbled. "But I did find a strange-looking seashell the other day."

Lumi wriggled in Ellabeth's pocket. "It's probably the element," he whispered.

"Can you show me where it is?" she asked. "If I find what I'm looking for, I can go and never return."

"Never?" the monster said. "But I like talking to you."

"There's no pleasing some monsters," Ellabeth joked. "One minute you want to eat me and the next you want to talk."

The monster chuckled. "You're funny, little mouse," he said. "I wish I had more friends like you." He waddled over to his cave and reached inside. "Is this what you're looking for?" He held up a yellow crystal shaped like a seashell.

Ellabeth could hardly believe her luck. Being nice had really worked.

"The air element," Ellabeth said as she held the crystal to her ear. She heard the sound of the wind shifting the trees. "Thank you. I'll go now and leave you in peace." She handed it to Lumi, who was still tucked inside her tunic, for safekeeping.

"You won't tell anyone that I'm not that scary, will you?" the monster asked.

"No," said Ellabeth.

"And you'll come back to visit one day?" asked the monster.

"I promise," Ellabeth said. "Now, I must check on my friend."

"Oh, yes," said the monster. "I hope she's okay," he gulped.

"So do I," Ellabeth said as she hurried back to Willow and the unicorns.

Willow was sitting up, rubbing her head. Obecky nudged her gently.

"What's happening?" Willow mumbled.

As Ellabeth helped Willow to her feet, she cast a worried eye at the clouds gathering over the mainland. The air cooled, and the wind picked up.

"Good news is I've recovered the air element," Ellabeth said. "Bad news is I don't have time to explain what happened."

"How come?" Willow asked.

"Because there's a huge storm coming," Ellabeth said, nodding toward the coast. "You're not doing that, are you, Lumi?" she asked the sprite.

"Not me," Lumi replied innocently.

The girls studied the sky above the Avamayan coastline. Giant clouds marched toward the ocean, shadowing the hills near the beach.

"Why do those clouds look like they're alive?" Willow asked.

Realization dawned on Ellabeth. "Because they're not clouds," she said. "They're masses of fly-by-night raptors. They shouldn't be out during the day. They hunt only at night."

"There are so many," Willow murmured. "They're blocking the sun."

Ellabeth's heart caught in her chest. "Valerian must want Lumi badly if he's sent such a force," she said.

"If Valerian controls the weather," Willow said, "he controls crops, food supplies, and people. He controls everything."

Ellabeth felt Lumi shiver. "Well, if he wants Lumi, he has to come through us first," she declared, hoping to reassure the sprite. "We need to get back to the others."

The girls leaped onto their unicorns and steered them into the ocean.

"Where are Krystal and Quinn?" Ellabeth asked. She scanned the beach as they swam back to the mainland. "I can't see them."

The birds swarmed closer. Ellabeth saw their red glowing eyes and heard their shrieks. Through the trees, Krystal and Quinn appeared, riding at full speed and being chased by enormous fly-by-nights. The raptors tore at the girls' clothing and hair. They scratched the unicorns' backs with their talons.

"Come on, girl, they need our help," Ellabeth told Fayza.

Obecky and Fayza raced out of the waves and up the beach.

"Use your light magic!" Ellabeth cried.

Fayza sent a burst of brilliant light from her topaz horn. It was so blinding, Ellabeth had to look away. The fly-by-nights chasing Krystal and Quinn screeched and dropped to the ground, dazed and disoriented.

More came to replace them. Handfuls of the giant birds swooped down from the sky, shrieking angrily and attacking the Unicorn Riders.

"Estrella, use your enchantment magic," Krystal said.

Estrella rose onto her back legs and began dancing. Pearly-white magic spun from her horn. Several terrifying moments passed as the girls watched and waited. Estrella's magic battled the ferocious birds until finally they succumbed to the enchantment. Quinn urged Ula to send the birds away with her mind powers. The raptors turned and headed inland.

"Go home!" Ellabeth yelled after them. "Go before we turn you into dinner."

"And stay away!" Lumi yelled as he appeared out of the top of Ellabeth's tunic, shaking his fist.

"Did you get the third element?" Quinn asked Ellabeth.

"She sure did," Lumi said, touching his pouch. "I'm almost whole again."

"What happened on the island?" Krystal asked.

"We'll ride now," Willow said. "Talk later."

"But the fly-by-nights hurt the unicorns," Krystal said. "They need their wounds taken care of."

"You took a bad knock to your head, too," Ellabeth told Willow.

"We should put some distance between us and the fly-by-nights in case they return," Willow said. "Obecky's magic will keep the unicorns strong while we ride."

"And Fayza will help us travel fast," Ellabeth said as she patted her unicorn.

"Where are we heading?" Willow asked Lumi.

The sprite glowed red. "There's only one place the fire element could be," he said. "It's the hottest part of Avamay."

"Ula's sending me a mind-picture of flames and lava," Quinn said. "Is it The Fire Line volcanoes?"

Lumi clapped his hands. "That's it," he said.

"Right," Willow said. "We know our destination. Do we ride as one?"

"We ride as one!" the girls cheered.

• CHAPTER 9 •

THE RIDERS SKIRTED THE volcanoes forming The Fire Line. They took the track that snaked around the base of the craters. Ellabeth had traveled along here many times as a young child before becoming a Rider.

I wish I was visiting for fun, she thought to herself. *Not under these dangerous circumstances.*

Lumi poked his head out of Ellabeth's pocket. "What is it?" Ellabeth asked.

"I sense the element in the middle volcano," Lumi replied.

The middle volcano was the smallest but steepest of the three. It hadn't erupted for years, although it was still active. Ellabeth and the others rode their unicorns to the top and peered over the edge. It was a long way down. In the center of the volcano rose a rock pedestal resembling a tower.

"There," Lumi said. "On top of that tower."

"The only way to get up there is to go down the volcano first and then scale up the rock tower," Ellabeth said.

"Those walls are so steep," Krystal said. "How will we get down there?"

"You could lower me down with my lasso," Ellabeth suggested.

"All right. Let's give it a shot," Willow said.

Ellabeth sat Lumi on Fayza's back. Willow, Krystal, and Quinn held one end of her lasso while Ellabeth tied the other end around her waist and lowered herself down into the volcano. It was difficult work. She had to search carefully for decent footholds. Her arms and legs strained from supporting her weight. It had been ages since she'd done any rock climbing.

She felt clumsy and awkward. Several times she had to stop for a sip of water.

When she reached the bottom, Ellabeth started climbing the rock tower. Once her grip slipped, and she almost fell. She was losing her nerve and was wanting to give up. Her hands were scratched and sweaty. Her fingernails were torn. Dirt and pebbles had fallen into her hair and covered her uniform.

Keep climbing, she told herself. *Keep climbing.*

Eventually, Ellabeth reached the top of the rock tower. Bursting with pride and panting from exertion, she pulled herself up and held her arms wide. "I did it!" she exclaimed.

"Well done," Willow called from the volcano rim. "Can you see the element?"

Ellabeth searched around. "It's not here!" she snapped tiredly. "Are you sure it was the middle volcano?"

"There's no need to shout. It's not my fault," Lumi shouted back. His angry mood made the sun hotter.

Ellabeth stomped around, grumbling to herself, until she heard something clink under her boot. Bending down, she saw a red stone shaped like a flame.

She held it high to show the others. "This must be it," she said.

Lumi squealed. "Be careful!" he said.

"Okay, okay," Ellabeth said as she slipped the crystal into her pocket and began her descent down the rock tower. Halfway to the bottom, Ellabeth ran out of energy. She'd been climbing for over an hour and was completely exhausted. "My whole body's aching," she groaned. "I can't do it."

"Yes, you can," Willow insisted. "Fayza needs you. And Lumi needs his element. Come on."

She's right, Ellabeth thought. *You can do this.*

Somehow, Ellabeth found the strength to keep going. She reached the bottom of the tower and began climbing the volcano toward her friends.

"You're doing great," Krystal called from the top.

Ellabeth kept climbing. Soon cool hands wrapped around her wrists and dragged her over the rim.

"I'm sorry I shouted at you," Lumi whimpered.

Ellabeth handed the fire element to the sprite. "That's okay. Everything's going to be fine," she said.

Lumi took the other elements from his pouch and held all four in his hands. The crystals magically drew together like four points of a cross. One was black and shaped like an egg. One was aqua and shaped like a star. One was yellow and shaped like a seashell. And one was red and shaped like a flame. United as one, the four elements glowed brighter than ever.

Ellabeth and the other Riders stared in wonder.

Lumi chuckled as he pulled the elements apart and slipped them back into his pouch. "That's my party trick," he warbled. "Oh, it's so good to have them back. Thank you."

"The next stop is Zenna Castle, where we'll reunite Lumi with Kai Liang," Willow said.

"Yay!" Lumi cheered and clapped his hands.

Ellabeth squinted into the distance. "Oh, no! The fly-by-nights are back," she said. "And there are more than ever."

"Perhaps we should split up," Quinn suggested.

"I could take Lumi and the elements while you lead the fly-by-nights elsewhere," Ellabeth said. "If you shake them off, we can meet up at Zenna Castle."

"Let's do it," Willow said. "We'll each go in different directions to confuse them. Quinn and Krystal, I'll meet you at Keydell where we'll regroup and hopefully — if we've gotten rid of the raptors — set out for Zenna. Ellabeth, you take Lumi back to Kai Liang. Good luck, Riders."

Willow, Krystal, and Quinn rode off. A portion of the fly-by-nights followed each girl. Even though Lumi was tucked up inside her pocket, Ellabeth still felt lonely. But that didn't stop her.

Night fell. No matter how fast Fayza galloped, she couldn't shake the fly-by-nights. Ellabeth couldn't risk Fayza using her light magic. Not when she needed her to keep her strength up for riding. For hours, Ellabeth heard wings flapping overhead. Sometimes, the fly-by-nights swooped low. Other times, they screeched from afar. All the while they hounded her.

Tired and frightened, Ellabeth started crying. Until now, she'd always had either her sisters or the other Riders supporting her. She'd never faced danger alone.

I can't do this, she thought. *What if I get lost? Or caught?*

Tears splashed Ellabeth's cheeks and landed on Lumi.

"Is it raining?" he asked. "I'm getting soaked."

"Sorry," Ellabeth said as she swiped at her tears. "It's the fly-by-nights. They terrify me."

"Why would a clever, brave girl like you be afraid?" he asked. "You can do anything! Without you, I wouldn't have found my elements. Is there some way I can help? Perhaps I can make the wind chase those horrible birds away. It won't be as powerful as what Kai Liang could do, but I'll try."

"We have to do something," Ellabeth said. "I don't know how much longer we can keep going like this."

"Consider it done," Lumi said. "But make sure Fayza stays at the front of the storm. I wouldn't want to hurt her."

"Would that be okay, girl?" Ellabeth asked.

Fayza whinnied in response, galloping faster.

Ellabeth grasped Fayza's silky mane tightly. She leaned down low and whispered, "I knew you could do it. That's why I love you so much."

Lumi whipped up a ferocious wind. The fly-by-nights shrieked as they struggled to stay airborne. The wind soon blew them away.

Fayza cantered on throughout the night. Before long, enormous mountains towered in the distance. The road split into four paths. Ellabeth knew only one led to Zenna. But which one was it?

● CHAPTER 10 ●

ELLABETH INDICATED FOR FAYZA to stop. She took Lumi from her pocket. "Which path should we take?" she asked.

"Thinking, thinking," the sprite said as he paced circles on Ellabeth's hand. "Kai Liang always said a rhyme when we came to these paths."

"Can you remember it?" Ellabeth coaxed.

"Let me see. . . . Four paths into the mountains I know, yet one only to Zenna does flow. Right can be overlooked without fear." Ellabeth pointed to each track as Lumi recited the lines. "Next to right leads the traveler back here. Left is almost right, though still not true. Second to left is spot-on, if Zenna is for you."

"It has to be this one," Ellabeth said. "Second from the left. Is that right?"

"Right," Lumi said. "I mean, left. Or second from the left. Correct?"

Ellabeth giggled. "Correct," she said.

They followed the trail until they came to a clear blue river that reflected the sky above. The moonlight was so incredibly bright, Ellabeth could see everything as clearly as if it were daylight. Emerald conifers, golden maples, and pink cherry blossoms grew on the river's banks. Beyond the river, mauve-colored mountains were capped with pearly snow.

Ellabeth stared. "It's every color of the rainbow," she said.

"That's why it's called the Rainbow River," Lumi said as he pointed to a stone castle sitting on top of the famed Glass Mountain. It was named because of the volcanic glass, or obsidian, that covered it. "That's Zenna," Lumi said. "We're almost there."

They soon reached a stone archway marking the start of a long staircase stretching toward Zenna. Ellabeth dismounted to lead Fayza up the stairs. She quickly lost count of the steps they'd climbed.

Next, they came to a walkway snaking toward the castle gates.

"It's so peaceful here," Ellabeth said as she stepped onto the path as she admired the view.

"Wait!" Lumi cried.

The path shimmered and shifted. It broke into pieces and then magically united again to form a giant stone dog with black eyes and sharp teeth.

Fayza snorted with fear.

"Oh, dear, I should have warned you," Lumi said.

"Bad dog!" Ellabeth shouted. "Sit down. Sit!"

The dog growled as it stalked closer.

Ellabeth stretched herself to her full height. "Stop barking right now," she commanded. "Sit!"

The dog crouched on its haunches, preparing to attack.

This isn't working, Ellabeth thought. *What am I doing wrong?* She took a deep breath as she searched inside herself for the answer.

Perhaps if I'm gentle with him, he might respond, she thought.

"Good boy," Ellabeth murmured. "Down boy. We're not going to hurt you. Good boy."

The dog stopped growling and lowered its head.

Ellabeth patted the dog's muzzle. "You like that, don't you?" she whispered. "You're not scary at all. Stay now. Stay."

The dog rested its giant head on its paws and lay still. Within seconds, it had become the stone path once more. Once inside the castle gates, Ellabeth saw the place was a mess. Walls were crumbled, rubbish lay scattered everywhere, and gardens were choked with weeds. No one had been looking after Zenna Castle for some time.

Fayza was exhausted from her race up the mountain, and her magic was depleted. Ellabeth left her in the courtyard while she and Lumi searched for Kai Liang. The sprite fluttered orange. "I hope my master is here," he said worriedly.

They eventually found the wizard in a room high up in a turret. He was asleep in bed. The room was cold and drafty. No fire had been lit.

Ellabeth shook Kai Liang awake.

"Where am I?" he asked.

"You're at Zenna," Ellabeth replied. "I'm returning Lumi to you."

The wizard's eyes shone. "Luminari! My light!" he said. "I thought I'd lost you forever. Thank goodness you're home."

Lumi jumped into Kai Liang's arms, glowing purple and purring happily.

Leaving Lumi and his master to get reacquainted, Ellabeth traipsed down to the kitchen in search of food. All she found were two potatoes, an onion, and some wilted herbs.

"These will have to do," she said.

She made potato soup and carried it back upstairs. While Kai Liang ate, Ellabeth lit a fire in the grate.

"Thank you. That's the first thing I've eaten in days," Kai Liang said. "I'm afraid I'm not able to look after myself, or Zenna Castle, as well as I used to."

Ellabeth heard shrieking. She looked out the window. A swarm of fly-by-nights was heading toward Zenna. Leading the flock was Gelsan. He was riding an eelios, a flying serpent who could spit deadly venom.

Ellabeth ran to fetch Fayza. She led her up into the turret. The unicorn's hooves clip-clopped tiredly up the stairs. With Kai Liang's help, Ellabeth pushed the dresser and wardrobe against the windows. She left one tiny gap where she could look out.

Ellabeth spied a bow and some arrows hanging on the wall. She took them down and checked them. It wouldn't be much against several thousand raptors, but it was all she had. Perhaps she could scare them away with a few well-aimed shots.

The fly-by-nights swooped, circling the turret, and searching for a way in. Ellabeth peered through the gap between the dresser and the window edge.

"We know you're in there," Gelsan called from outside. Riding on his eelios, he sat in line with the window. "Hand over the sprite and we won't harm you. My master, Lord Valerian, would like the pleasure of his company." Gelsan laughed wickedly.

Ellabeth fired an arrow in Gelsan's direction. It shot over his head, just as she'd intended. Gelsan looked shaken at the near miss, but remained seated on his eelios.

"Do you have any magic that can help us?" Ellabeth asked the wizard.

"My magic is not what it used to be," Kai Liang admitted. "Long ago, I possessed enough power to protect Zenna from outsiders. All I have now is Lumi and the magical stone dog. Unfortunately, he can't fight intruders from the sky."

Lumi fluttered around Kai Liang trying to comfort him.

Gelsan shouted orders to the fly-by-nights. "Tear the place apart!" he said.

The raptors obeyed, ripping at the castle with their talons and beaks. It wouldn't be long before they'd break through the walls.

If only the other Riders were here, Ellabeth thought. *I need their help.*

Ellabeth pulled the bowstring back. Her second arrow flew past Gelsan's ear. He jerked his head away. The movement made him lose his balance. He tumbled off his eelios to the bricks below.

Afraid to let her precious unicorn out of her sight, Ellabeth took Fayza with her as she raced down the stairs. Their only chance was to capture Gelsan before he remounted.

• CHAPTER 11 •

AS ELLABETH RAN INTO the courtyard with Fayza, she saw the fly-by-nights still circling overhead and attacking the castle.

Gelsan lay on the bricks. "I've sprained my ankle," he moaned.

"Here, doggy!" Ellabeth called. "Good doggy. Come here. I need you."

The stone path shimmered and shook until it magically transformed into the huge dog again.

"That's it. Good," Ellabeth said as she patted him. "Can you guard this boy for me?"

The dog woofed obediently and advanced on Gelsan.

"Please don't hurt me," Gelsan whimpered.

The sound of clattering hooves made Ellabeth turn. Willow, Krystal, and Quinn cantered into the courtyard.

Ellabeth hugged each of them as they dismounted. "I'm so glad to see you," she said.

"Sorry it took us so long," Willow apologized. "We had trouble finding the right trail."

"And we had to battle the raptors when they spotted us approaching," Krystal said. "Estrella was magnificent as usual."

Kai Liang appeared, carrying Lumi. Ellabeth introduced him to everyone.

"Gelsan and his feathered friends have been causing trouble, as you can see," Ellabeth said. She tied her lasso around Gelsan's wrists. "Your ankle doesn't look too bad," she told him. "We'll attend to it in a minute. First, I want to see if Fayza's recovered enough to blast those fly-by-nights. Her magic is still weak, but with Obecky's help it might work."

Fayza shot rays of light across the sky. Obecky's magic made the blasts stronger. The fly-by-nights shrieked and whirled about, disoriented and confused. After several blasts, the birds scattered. The sky was clear once more.

"Great teamwork," Willow congratulated Obecky and Fayza.

The stone dog barked. Ellabeth saw Gelsan had untied the lasso and was limping toward Kai Liang.

"Look out!" Ellabeth cried.

Gelsan knocked Kai Liang down and seized Lumi. The terrified sprite gurgled and turned red. Clouds formed overhead as thunder rumbled.

"Help me!" Lumi yelled.

"Now, weather sprite, how would you like to work for a real wizard?" Gelsan asked. "My master wants to make far better use of you than Kai Liang can."

Lumi clutched his pouch to his chest. "I'd rather be extinguished forever than work for Lord Valerian."

"You're not taking Lumi anywhere," Ellabeth said.

Gelsan snatched Lumi and held the sprite high. "I control you now that I have you and your elements together," he said. "Lord Valerian told me you're unable to resist the combined elemental powers. You must be a servant to whomever possesses you. So, sprite, cover these Riders with ice so they freeze to the spot. Then I'll take you to your new master."

Lumi shot Ellabeth an apologetic look. He lifted his hands. Ellabeth racked her brain for a way to help the sprite.

"What's wrong?" Gelsan shouted at Lumi. "I told you to freeze them."

While Gelsan was distracted, Ellabeth motioned to Fayza. The unicorn hit Gelsan with a blast of light that brought him to his knees.

Ellabeth grabbed Lumi. "I'll take him, thank you very much," she said.

A screech sounded overhead. The eelios had returned. It swooped down, and Gelsan leaped onto its back. "Next time, Riders, I *will* beat you," he declared as he flew away.

"I hope there isn't a next time!" Quinn shouted after him.

"Knowing Valerian, there will be," Ellabeth said as she kicked the bricks. "I wish Gelsan hadn't gotten away."

"At least he didn't get Lumi," Willow said.

Ellabeth held the sprite close to her face. "Why didn't you work for Gelsan?" she asked. "I thought you had to obey whomever held your four elements."

"I may have overlooked telling you the complete story on that," Lumi said. "Very few people know that I don't have just four elements. There are actually five. Gelsan could never control me. Not until he learns the secret fifth element."

"Which is?" Ellabeth asked.

"Compassion," Lumi said, touching Ellabeth's chest. "That element can only be found in a kind person's heart. You showed me, the monster on

Granite Island, Kai Liang's dog, and even Gelsan compassion. The elements I keep respond to my master's compassion. They work together to control nature itself. The weather patterns I created in Cardamon are nothing compared to the magic Kai Liang was once able to perform."

"All the more reason for you both to be protected," Krystal observed.

Lumi bowed. "Ellabeth, when Kai Liang is no longer able to care for me, I hope you can be my new master," he said.

"Thank you, but I'm a Unicorn Rider," Ellabeth said as she stared at her boots. "I like being your friend, but I could never be your master. Something like that would take years to learn."

"Or you could be born with the knowledge," Quinn said.

Suddenly, they saw a man running toward them.

"I saw the fly-by-nights and the lights. Where's my father? Is he all right?" the man asked.

"Are you Tellarian?" Ellabeth asked.

"Yes," the man said. "My father asked me to take Lumi, but I was afraid of his powers. My wife convinced me to change my mind. I came as quickly as I could."

Kai Liang embraced Tellarian.

"Father, are you all right? Can you forgive me?" Tellarian asked.

"There's nothing to forgive," Kai Liang said, smiling. "But I do have much to teach you, my son."

"I wish only to be as good a wizard as you've been," Tellarian said.

"What do you think?" Ellabeth whispered to Lumi. "Do you see compassion in Tellarian's heart?"

"I do," Lumi said as he glowed purple.

"So do I," Ellabeth said, grinning.

• CHAPTER 12 •

ELLABETH STOOD WITH THE other Riders and their unicorns in the courtyard of Zenna Castle. "We know we're leaving you in good hands," Ellabeth told Lumi. "But I'm going to miss you."

Lumi glowed blue. "I'm going to miss you, too," he said sadly.

"You took us on quite an adventure," said Willow.

"I'm sorry we caused such a fuss," Kai Liang said. "Everything seems so much harder now than when I was young."

"That's why I'm here," Tellarian said. "You never have to worry again." He turned to the Riders. "We won't give you any further trouble either."

"It was no problem, really," Quinn said.

"What if Gelsan returns with his fly-by-nights?" Krystal asked. "How will you protect yourselves?"

"We won't stay here," Tellarian said. "Zenna Castle served father well, but I need somewhere my family can be happy. We'll find a new home, somewhere unknown to Valerian. I will let you know when we've settled in."

"Excellent idea," Quinn said.

Willow and Krystal agreed.

Ellabeth stepped toward Tellarian. She held her hands out. "May I?" she asked.

Lumi jumped into Ellabeth's embrace. He hugged her neck, his short arms almost reaching all the way around as his tiny transparent form glowed purple. "I won't forget you," he purred.

"I won't forget you either," Ellabeth said as she rubbed her eye. "Silly wind. It's blowing dust everywhere."

Krystal laughed and hugged Ellabeth. "Come on, you still have us," they said.

"I know," Ellabeth said. She sniffed as she handed Lumi back to Tellarian. Then she and the other Riders mounted their unicorns and rode away.

Two days later, they were back at the Unicorn Riders' estate in Keydell where they were reunited with their leader.

"I'm so glad you're all okay," Jala said. She greeted the girls and then steered them into the kitchen. "So, another successful mission completed."

"Thanks mostly to Ellabeth," Willow said. "She showed amazing bravery."

"You should have seen her with Lumi," Quinn said. "She was so gentle and caring."

Ellabeth blushed. "I'm just glad it all worked out in the end," she said.

"Here, here," Willow cheered.

"And now, for the best bit," Jala said. "I asked Alda to make her special strawberry swirl sponge cake to celebrate your return."

"Yum!" Ellabeth said. "That's my favorite."

Krystal rolled her eyes. "What are you talking about? Every one of Alda's cakes is your favorite," she said.

"Well . . . ," Ellabeth said, giggling as Jala handed her some cake. "I have to admit, you've got me there."

Glossary

depleted (di-PLEET-id)—emptied or used up

deserted (di-ZUR-tid)—empty of people; without anyone

detour (DEE-toor)—a different, usually longer way to go somewhere when the direct route is closed or blocked

devastation (DEV-uh-stay-shuhn)—severe damage or destruction

klutz (KLUHTZ)—a clumsy person

nuisance (NOO-suhns)—someone or something that is annoying or causes problems

paddock (PAD-uhk)—an enclosed field or area

precariously (pri-KAIR-ee-uhsly)—not in a secure position

regiment (REJ-uh-muhnt)—a military unit of two or more battalions

soothe (SOOTH)—to gently calm someone who is angry or upset

stalactites (stuh-LAK-tytes)—growths that hang from the ceiling of a cave and were formed by dripping water

stalagmites (stuh-LAG-mytes)—growths that stand on the floor of a cave and were formed by drips of water from above

turret (TUR-it)—round or square towers on a castle, usually on a corner

Discussion Questions

1. Why was this mission so meaningful to Ellabeth?

2. How did Ellabeth take charge of finding the four elements?

3. What is Lumi feeling when he turns purple? What makes you think that?

Writing Prompts

1. Why do you think Ellabeth is so protective of Lumi? Why does she open up to him?

2. Ellabeth took off from the rest of the group more than once. Do you think this was a good idea? Why or why not?

3. Lumi's fifth element was compassion. How did Ellabeth show compassion throughout the book?

UNICORN RIDERS

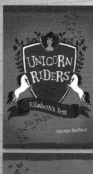

Ellabeth's Test

Aleesah Darlison

Krystal's Choice

Aleesah Darlison

Quinn's Riddles

Aleesah Darlison

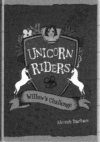

Willow's Challenge

Aleesah Darlison

Quinn's Truth

Aleesah Darlison

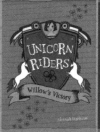

Willow's Victory

Aleesah Darlison

Ellabeth's Light

Aleesah Darlison

Krystal's Charge

Aleesah Darlison

COLLECT THE SERIES!